DISCLAIMER

Thank you so much for your support! Please be aware that this is an EARLY ACCESS version of the final installment of the Fight for Survival series. Although these chapters are pretty solidified, there is still room for subtle changes and slight differences from the official published version.

12 YEARS AGO

THE PLANS FOR OUR HEADQUARTERS to be built into Mt. Diablo have been approved. By this time next year, our quiet takeover will be deep seated in nature, hidden in plain sight. Thankfully, dear old daddy bought my pitch and I was able to finally weasel my way into his life.

Speaking of fathers…

"Mistress," some nameless friend of my father's calls over the radio. He anointed him Sergeant Major of the new American Liberation Force. Another of my ideas he feels the need to take credit for. "A gentlemen named Paul Warin would like to see you."

Paul. It's been thirteen years since I've seen him. Thirteen years since I've seen our son. I knew it was only a matter of time before he'd seek me out. I am, in fact, a well-known public figure now. I wonder how Lucas is, how they're doing. Did Paul tell him wonderful stories of me? By now, he should be a strong young man. Soon he'll be capable of leading great armies and taking control of any situation thrown his way. I can't wait to get reacquainted.

"Bring him up."

I don't often get flutters in my chest, but the thought of seeing Paul leaves me almost giddy. Or maybe it's the fact that I'm powerful now. When Paul found me, I was just a shadow of a human being, tossed aside like the garbage I was. Then again, Paul was dealing with his own demons.

What a power couple we'll be; what a powerful family we'll be all together again.

"Ren." The man from my past is standing in the middle of my office now. *My* office.

"Paul," I answer back, a slight smirk playing at my lips. "How have you been?"

His face morphs into a painful expression. Or maybe it's anger. I've always been good at reading people, but not Paul. "How have I been?" he questions. "What do you care? You left! What the hell are you doing here?"

I'm taken off guard. His temper had always been even. "Is that any way to greet your wife? You know why I'm here. No more suffering. No more faults. We're going to make Humanity better. You, me, and Lucas."

"My wife?" He's shocked. "You left!" he repeats. "You left and never turned back."

Paul has completely ignored my plans. We used to talk about fixing the flaws of Humanity together. No poor, no different, no suffering. Everything—everyone—equal. And now, here he is, completely ignoring our dream.

I open my mouth to speak, but he cuts me off.

"Don't even argue. Janet is my wife. You are just the ghost of my past," he spits. "So what are you *really* doing? Combining the houses? It's one thing to talk about a future without flaws for our son, but it's another to completely take control of the very system that keeps us safe."

"Safe?" I cry, losing my composure momentarily. "That same system that left me to starve? Left me to rot while my bitch of a mother got high? Left *you* an orphan to fend for yourself?"

Much to his consternation, he continues, wiping all emotion away. "These unresolved problems with your parents are exactly why you don't deserve to see Lucas after all this time. I've made my peace," he spits. "And that's why I'm here. To come to an agreement."

Irritation surges through my veins. Fine, the man I love has moved on with some trollop named Janet, but Lucas is *my* son. He is the one that will carry on the legacy after I'm gone. "Why the hell not? He is still my son, isn't he? Or did Janet take some claim over him?" The way her name tastes in my mouth makes me want to vomit.

"Pfft." Paul chuckles flippantly. "You don't deserve him because of what you've done. Sure, talk about change all you want. But you said you wanted to be different than your parents."

"I am different," I say. How could he think otherwise? I'm taking control like my father, sure, but at least I'm making a difference.

"No," he derides. "You're not. You left for something better rather than making it. You're just like John. Hiding the parts you were disappointed in. And what, did you blackmail him for this cushy new position?"

The insinuation of the fact that I didn't earn every bit of this sends anger straight into my chest, rage filling it quickly. As if I'm not *making* things better currently. But I'm the Headmistress now. I need to make myself appear calm, even if I'm red hot and boiling on the inside. "I planned on seeing Lucas, yes. Once things died down a bit. I'm surprised he hasn't already asked to see me."

Paul is silent. His features are stoic. His eyes are the eyes of my sweet Lucas, but they are troubled.

"What?" I question, squinting.

There's hardly any hesitation from Paul. "He believes you're dead."

"Excuse me?" This time it's harder to hold my composure. Fiery rage billows through every pore.

"You left us, Ren! You broke my heart. I wasn't going to give our son some sense of false hope that you'd return."

"So you told him I died?" I can't believe this. What a sick asshole. How could he do that to our son? My little Lucas?

"Oh, that's rich," he says. "Should I have told him the truth? That you couldn't handle how imperfect he was? That you craved control? He was just a kid, Ren. He needed guidance, and you tossed him aside like you were as a kid."

His onslaught continues.

"I told him you moved to the East. That it was too far to see you. The Undoing... well..." His voice fades to almost nothing.

I back up until my backside rests against my desk. "How..."

"Take it as a blessing, Ren. At least he has a good reason to believe about why you weren't around."

Paul wants me to see the bright side here. At first, I can't. But suddenly, my face morphs into a smile at the thought. This is great! This is actually the best news I could receive. Lucas will be so excited to learn that I'm not dead. He'll be ecstatic to join the cause for some bonding time. My father, and my son, together, taking on the flaws of Humanity. He'll come around. The same way I did. He won't blame me for searching for something better.

How great! This is all I've ever wanted.

"What?" Paul's harsh tone tears my from my fantasy.

"Lucas will be so happy to reign by my side. To learn I'm not actually dead."

"You're not telling him," Paul says, calmly.

"What? Why?" The death of a parent makes for a strong individual. It's even better than I could have imagined. Lucas has to be perfect.

"He's a sixteen year old boy! He's already confused about things. He doesn't need this."

"A boy needs his mother!" I screech.

"Then you wouldn't have left us behind like we meant nothing!" Paul is in my face, screaming. Then, he takes a breath. "If you tell Lucas anything about your identity, Ren, so help me God I will kill him."

A gasp escapes my slightly parted lips. "You wouldn't," I breathe, but I know he means it. Paul is a straightforward man. He means what he says.

I feel the hotness of his breath on my face. "Watch me," he seethes. "I won't let you ruin my son." He steps back, our eyes holding onto each other, stuck in a battle of wills. "As long as my heart is beating, I will take everything you want from this world, believe me. Killing him would be merciful. So, give me your word."

An eternity of silence passes before I nod. "I won't tell Lucas who I am."

Paul nods, his face still pulled into an uncomfortably pained expression. He turns, ready to leave me just like I'd walked away all those years ago. I guess I don't blame him. But this new game, the thrill, is exciting to me. He may have the upper hand now, but he will not keep it.

Before Paul makes it to the door, I speak out. "I promise not to tell Lucas, but I still have big plans for him."

Paul doesn't fully turn around, but it's clear how rigid his body is. Adrenaline shoots through my very soul.

My next words are chosen carefully. "There will come a day where I will convince Lucas to kill you. And on that day, I will rejoice with my son."

CHAPTER ONE   AMITY

THE SOUNDS OF A HOSPITAL room are not the sounds I wish to hear. I want to hear my father read me his poetry. Emma's sweet giggle. Grace's funny jokes. I want to hear my mother's voice again. But instead I'm stuck drowning in medicinal beeps and IV drips.

In my head, in my heart, my mother has only been gone a month or so. Grace just a bit longer. But the doctors tell me it's been longer. Six years to be exact. They won't tell me where Emma is, though. Apparently she's not four. According to their timetable, a few months ago she turned ten. *How could I have lost so much of our life together?*

The doctors won't tell me where my father is, either. I just don't get it. What happened to me? To them? Something doesn't feel right about all of this, and instinctively my eyes search for the one they call Sarge. He's always here.

Laying on the love seat, the large, black beast watches over me. His golden eyes refuse to move from my direction. He doesn't lift his head, or blink. When I look at him, something flutters in my chest. His heart calls to mine in a way I'd never thought possible. I sit here in a hospital room, all broken, and yet I can somehow feel whole when Sarge is near.

They tell me he's mine. The best dog anyone can ask for. And it makes sense. He hasn't left this room for as long as I've been conscious. A dog potty station had to be added because he refuses to leave my side, even for that.

The truth is, I don't remember anything. I don't remember finding him in the woods, or my father letting me keep him. But when I look at Sarge, I believe it. We are tethered by a bond so unbreakable that the depth of it is unfathomable to the human mind. But it's not something you know in your head; it's something you feel in the deepest parts of your soul. And I felt it the second we locked eyes.

A commotion outside of my room pulls me from my thoughts. Pacing feet and the shuffle of something plasticky. Then a doctor—a voice I recognize—says, "You can't go in there!" before a tall, muscular man storms in, pulling back the curtain.

"Says who?" he answers, with a roll of his eyes. His lips twitch as he focuses his gaze on me.

This is Luke, or so they say. He's got a sharp and slanted nose, pronounced jawline, and gorgeous hazel eyes. But when I say that he's exasperating, I'm putting it mildly. He *rescued* me from the Reaver, I know that much. He's told me we were…something. Not friends, but….he won't be specific. He also told me that he'd take me to see Emma. So…

"Back again to lie to me?" My words are heavy, but the tone is playful. I'm making jokes at the expense of my fears.

Luke brushes off the subtle jab. "Here to give you flowers." He pulls a stem of three beautiful, yellow marigolds from behind his back. The gesture is sweet, but my eyes subconsciously flick to the giant, elegant bouquet that sits across the room. Luke's eyes follow, his neck tensing slightly. "But I see you don't need any more." His knuckles tense around the plastic pot and I find myself in a weird state.

Normally I wouldn't care how someone felt about such trivial things, but something about Luke is calling to me, telling me to make it right. Whatever that means. "No." I blush. "But I much prefer the simplicity of yours." I peek up through my lashes to see a shocked expression, followed by a smirk.

In such a short time, I've truly grown to like the playful guise that Luke takes on in small snippets. Yet, every time I get a tumbling chest over it, I chastise myself. Luke is someone I can't trust…yet. My mind is feeble right now, but I'll be damned if I let him in.

Luke walks toward the extravagant bouquet and places the marigolds in front of it. "The three stems signify you, me, and Sarge," he whispers, barely audible. *Shit.*

Heat flushes in my cheeks. How is anyone supposed to keep distance after that? All of the most alluring things are dangerous.

Luke turns, his hazels meeting my greys, and my face beats red once more. He holds the contact for a few, but then pulls away to look at his watch. He's agitated when he returns his gaze. "So, I lied," he speaks.

Point proven. Of course. Panic settles in my chest and Sarge lifts his head from the love seat. The action helps me stay calm. Maybe Luke should get the benefit of the doubt? *How could you, Amity? He's lied before. You know trust has to be earned.*

"I'm actually here to invite you to Axom and Charlotte's memorial tonight." The air changes harshly all at once with his words. Luke is no longer playful, there's no signature smirk anywhere close to his lips now. Only a deep-creased frown is present.

"The two that were with you that day?" I question. My brain is a fuzzy, but the last few days are still tucked away in my mind. This memory in particular I've tried to bury, but Luke's words force me to dig it back up.

Two people—two innocent people—getting crushed by crumbling stone. I can't help but feel that their deaths are somehow my fault. It's hard to fight my body's natural reaction to numb itself.

Luke nods. "I'd like it if you were there beside me." The hopeful look in his eyes sends a twinge to my heart, and my face softens. Then:

"Mr. Baines, he can't keep storming in like this!" The doctor's shrill voice pierces through the room.

"I'll handle it, Morin," a deep, dignified voice answers back. Then it's not just Luke in here anymore. It's the one they call Mason, too.

Mason Baines has a round, benevolent face. His dirty blonde hair is perfectly tussled atop his head, and he has these magnificent blue pools where eyes should be. When he talks, it makes me feel ready to take on the day.

Apparently, him and I were friends as well. I'm more inclined to believe him. After all, he hasn't lied to me yet…as far as I know. So I should give him some leniency? No. I shouldn't, really. Now is not the time for friendships. I lost Grace, and then my mom. Who else could I possibly be able to handle losing?

"Good morning, Amity." Mason smiles a kind smile at me. His plump lips pull back, and his perfect teeth come into view. His words cause visible disdain from Luke.

In the times this routine has played out, it's always a similar reaction. Luke bursts in, the doctors call Mason. Mason steps in to be the middle man, saying it's better him than getting the General involved. Luke makes a snide remark under his breath, and then they continue showing great disapproval of one another for the remainder of the event.

Forget dealing with my own history, I want to know theirs.

"Good morning." I nod. A small smile creeps onto my face. It's all I can muster up. "Luke was just inviting me to the memorial tonight?" I speak as though it's a question.

Mason subtly glares in Luke's direction. When his gaze returns to mine, it's as gentle as ever. "You really should be resting," he insists. His palm slides along the back of his neck. He's nervous. For some reason, he wants me to stay locked in this room. And just like that, I want to be everywhere but here.

"I think it would be better if I got up and moved around. Don't you agree, Luke?" Perhaps it would be good to learn more about my surroundings and those in it… not just the ones in this hospital ward.

Luke struggles to hide his smirk, but is able to keep his face serious as Mason turns to him. "Whatever the lady wants," he agrees. He winks at me once Mason returns his eyes to mine. I stifle a giggle.

"Fine," Mason ultimately acquiesces. "You'll need something to wear. I'll send it to you. But for now, you need rest."

Mason pulls Luke out of the room before I have a chance to say anything more. No goodbye or anything. They don't get far before Luke starts to argue, though. "What's your problem?"

Mason lets out a loud sigh. "You know we're not supposed to see her."

"Well that's stupid," Luke retorts. "We should be helping her!"

"We are!" Mason shouts, a little too loud. "Just because you don't understand, doesn't mean you can break all of the rules."

Luke switches gears. "You sent her flowers?" His voice sounds angrier than it should be over some smelly plants.

"Believe it or not, it's common practice to send flowers as get well soon gifts."

"Argh!" Luke answers with a grunting snort. "You did this shit on purpose!"

If they are trying to make it so I don't hear, they are failing miserably. But then, it gets so quiet that I almost believe they've walked away.

Their hushed, whispery yells intrigue me. I've been terribly bored and desperate for answers. So, I decide to sneak closer to the door. My bare feet barely make a noise as they touch the tiled floor. I go as far as the wires will allow.

"You have to look on the bright side," Mason whispers.

"What bright side, dipshit?" Luke spits back. "Amity can't stand me. Which is… fine." He gulps. "But she thinks I've lied to her. She won't trust me."

"You're grossly selfish," Mason replies. "She doesn't remember the death, the torture. You know what that means? There's no pain. No emotional scar left behind." *What?*

Torture? Death?

CHAPTER TWO AMITY

THE HUMAN PROTECTIVE SERVICE—WHICH is who I've come to know has taken me in—spares no expense for the memorials of their fallen soldiers. The young man and woman who had been with Luke as he rescued me are the first to be lost in a long time. There's no exception for memorializing them in the grandest way.

This is the first time I'll be up. The first time I'll be around people that aren't doctors. No hospital gowns, no wires, no isolation. Something deep inside me turns, the sensation leaving me sick to my stomach. Am I ready to face the world?

My mother wanted us to keep to the shadows; hide away, stay isolated. Exactly what Mason wants of me in this cell of a hospital room. So why do I feel it so deeply to get out? To put myself into the crowd?

Just then, Sarge moves. He makes his way from the love seat over to my bed, and he rests his chin on the soft sheets. His golden eyes make me feel safe. He's telling me it will be alright, that my decision is the right one. *Okay, Amity. You can face the world.*

One of the doctors had dropped off a box wrapped in a bow. They said I'd need to be ready for a grand ball of sorts. I've never been to one before, and I've been too nervous to even look in the box. But this is how they honor the dead here: Host a great gala in remembrance of all they've done to celebrate their life and honor their death. It's admirable, I suppose, though, nerve-wracking nonetheless. How does everyone have such a good time with the reminder of Death plaguing the air?

Regardless, the one called Luke will be here soon. He'll come, and I'll accompany him for the night. Normally this would leave a feeling of disdain to settle in my chest, but perhaps there is more to him than I originally thought. Luke is convinced he was forced to lie to me, that he never intended to hurt me or do it of his own volition. Couple that with the fact that the *lie* in question is concerning my sweet little M, and my mind is whirring with a tornado of all sorts of emotions.

Sarge backs up as I sling the sheets off my body, but doesn't go far. The air is slightly cold on my now exposed legs. My body somehow carries me toward the box, Sarge heeling perfectly, tightly pressed against my side. I'm shaking from nerves as I stop in front of the full body mirror. I've not seen myself since I don't know when. The word *torture* swirls to the forefront of my brain. Is it really possible I was tortured?

My fingers tremor as I undo the buttons behind my back. Dressing in hospital garb is definitely not flattering at all. Before the cloth falls to the ground, I jerk my gangly frame away from the glass, startling Sarge. My heart races, yet I attempt to keep my breathing under control. I don't want to see my whole body exposed. Not yet. *Maybe put the dress on first, Amity. Then try.*

The box is untied and the dress is pulled out in a matter of seconds. Sarge sits patiently behind me while I study the garment. It's a long, silver dress with thin straps. I'm hesitant as I slide the fabric over my body, but it's silky against my skin. There's never been a time where I've dressed up. Even when I was trying to project a higher status among the Slums, there was never anything this fancy in my closet.

Taking a deep breath, I try pooling all of my courage. I need to look at myself, but I'm worried I won't recognize the person that stares back. Will she be covered in cuts and bruises? Will her eyes be devoid of light? Will she look…sad? After a few seconds, I reach my hand out to summon Sarge. If I'm going to take this next step, then maybe it will help if I've got someone solid by my side.

Sarge's tail wags in excitement as he nudges his face against my hip. My hands explore the soft fur of his head and his eyes close in appreciation. How can I not remember such a wonderful creature? I can only imagine that he'd helped me through my mother's death the first time, and now he'll be here to do it again...

We step forward as one toward the mirror, my heart beating wildly in my chest. This is it. One last breath escapes my lips before everything is suspended. My eyes scan over my body. I'm thin, sort of sickly looking. My grey eyes are dull, and my hair is slightly matted in the back. There are tiny circular scars—barely noticeable—covering my chest, shoulders, neck. *Could this be a small sign of a torturous path?*

It's not long of me studying the scars before my eyes catch on a deeply pigmented symbol on my right arm, just below my shoulder. It's a delicate, black mark on my otherwise clean skin. It's...beautiful.

"Signal blocking ink," a voice states from behind me. My body jumps in reaction to being startled. "Sorry," Luke says.

"What's it blocking?" I ask, ignoring my nervousness. As much as I want answers, I hate to admit that I'm just as equally terrified of what will come to light.

Luke stares at me with an intense gaze. It appears his own nervous look settles into his pupils as he says, "Your tracker." Something deep within in my gut tells me this information should hold more weight to me. *A tracker?* If it's being blocked, I can't imagine it came from the H.P.S.. I scan my memories for the eight hundredth time trying to find a connection, but fail anew.

I open my mouth to ask more, but a different voice fills the air. *Damn it. Left without answers, again.*

"You look stunning." It's Mason.

Sarge lets out a muffled gruff as Mason gets closer. Like a warning. Mason doesn't come any closer. *Hello?* Is this a signal everyone knows? Sarge is probably the only one I wholeheartedly trust in this place. And something about Mason has set him off.

"Thank you," I say. My face flushes with embarrassment as his eyes subtly scan my body.

Luke radiates intensity. "I was under the impression that M and I would be alone." Luke sighs. *Did he just call me M?* Oh, right. For some reason he had done if before, too. An odd emotion sweeps across my chest…

There's a feeling through the room that seems off. I can't quite put my finger on the animosity. I never could, but this is far worse than any of the other spats I've bore witness to.

"I had to bring Sarge his tie," Mason admits.

A quick glance in Sarge's direction shows his eyes holding the same wariness that's settled in my chest. *Oh, how I wish he could talk.*

Mason hands the bow tie to Luke—a strange, out of place gesture. Luke asks if I'd prefer to do the honors myself. I nod and he steps forward. Listening for any trifle from Sarge, the room is quiet as Luke closes the distance. *Interesting.*

Our fingers touch as he places the bow tie in my hand, sending electricity shooting into my chest. *What the?* I ignore the feeling and awkwardly brush my hair behind my ear, turning away from him to deal with Sarge. I wish I understood what was happening. I wish I had at least *some* memory of the last six years.

Sarge smiles up at me, sitting tall and pretty, while I fasten the bow tie into his thick chest fur. He's a dapper gentleman next to me when I inspect us both in the mirror. The shimmery silk of the tie matches the silver of my dress. The sight calms me. Any unease that creeps into my heart is being combatted by Sarge's presence. *Perhaps tonight won't be so bad.*

I spin around and Sarge presses against me. The men gaze at me with the same expression: Admiration. Only, Luke's eyes hold sorrow in them, too. But when I look at him this time, an image shoots into my head, causing a sharp pain inside my skull. There's a man with a buzz cut standing in front of me. When I blink, he's gone. Replaced by Luke, who, I'm now realizing, has a similar style of hair. Or lack there of. What was that? *Or rather, who?*

"You okay?" Luke is genuinely concerned.

"Should we get going?" I ask, innocently. I decide to keep this little vision to myself. At least until I figure out who truly is on my side. If everyone wants to keep my past from me, then I'll be damned if I openly share my present. *Is anyone here even trustworthy at all?*

Luke nods, not quite convinced. Mason says he'll lead the way. There's no need to do an in-depth observation to see the pure and utter disdain this causes Luke to radiate. His body is tense, his gait is rigid. Mason escorts, Sarge and I follow. Luke brings up the rear. His eyes soften a bit when I peek back at him. For now, I believe him. Oddly enough, I do. And we want the same thing: to be alone.

Luke seems to know things, and by all things lucky, he wants me to know things, too. This means we have similar interests because I think I want to know everything he'll tell me. Perhaps it will be a lie, or perhaps that's just what Mason wants me to think. But it's the best place to start.

Mason leads us through the medical ward and out into, what I gather, is H.P.S Headquarters. Everything is hi-tech and clean; a stark contrast to the Slums of Western America. The pristine nature of the halls is vaguely familiar, but I can't place why. Never in a million years would I have guessed I'd see something this grand. I just wish my family were here to see it, too.

My hand finds Sarge's soft fur as we enter the grand ballroom. There's a large stage in the far right, food and drink along the back left, with what looks like a thousand people in between—and almost every single one of them is staring at us.

Anxiety pushing up into my chest, Sarge snakes his head around my hip, pressing himself closer. Mason is now to my right, with Sarge in between us, and Luke is slightly behind us to my left.

Perhaps this was a mistake. Maybe Mason was right, I should be resting.

"General Favager will be happy to meet you," Mason shouts over the loud din of the room. "Shall we find him?" He holds out his hand, expecting me to take it. The question was asked, but I feel I don't really have a choice. I don't need to turn around to see the anger coming from Luke because it's already palpable from a distance.

"I..." I hesitate, "You think maybe Luke could take me for a drink first?" My words surprise me, but it's Mason's expression that shocks me even more. It's so subtle that I almost don't see it, but his eyes flash frustration and distrust. It's gone after a second or two, no trace it was there in the first place.

"No problem," he says, his smile not quite reaching his eyes. "I'll bring the General to the refreshments table." He walks away, but not before shooting a glare in Luke's direction. I pretend not to notice.

"Shall we?" My eyes flick to Luke's as I turn around. My palm is still buried in the thickness of Sarge's fur, but Luke's playful smirk offers me some semblance of confidence.

"Yes, please!"

It takes about two seconds to realize that my worries of a crowded room are for naught. The swarm of bodies parts and clears a path for Sarge and I as we walk. Perhaps it's Sarge who scares them. *Or maybe it's me...*

We get to the refreshments table quicker than I anticipated. No one got in our way, no awkward shimmying passed bodies had to ensue. Luke asks what I'm in the mood for. *Answers,* I think, but I tell him water because he's referring to a drink. As he fills my cup and hands it to me, I probe for what I'm really after.

"The people here must be scared of us to move out of the way like that."

Luke's body tenses, a tell-tale sign that I've broached a sensitive subject. "I think it's more because of how bad I must smell." He shrugs, not missing a beat. The normality of it throws me off guard, and my lip twitches with the hint of a small smile.

"I suppose that makes sense," I say. "You reek."

Luke turns to me now with a hint of adoration in his eyes. Then, it gets torn away and replaced with some other emotion I can't quite pinpoint. Sorrow? Maybe grief?

"What's wrong?" I question.

"This... reminds me of a conversation we've had before."

"About how smelly you are?" I'm slightly confused. What an odd thing to talk about.

Luke chuckles a sad sound laugh. "Actually, yes."

The simplicity of this moment is bittersweet. Before Grace passed, and then my mother, I would have reveled in this type of normal. Yet, the thought of being close to anyone constricts my heart. What happened to make me change? If Luke is telling the truth, then I opened myself up to something more.

I know I should be finding answers about where my family is and what's happened to me, but maybe we can take a brief detour and learn about my mysterious past with this man.

"So you and I really were...something?" Luke may have lied to me before, but this particular tidbit appears to be backed up by the way he looks at me.

"Yes," he says, his face serious now. "M, I..." He reaches out his thick hand, gently brushing against my chest as he attempts to wipe the hair away, tucking it behind my ear.

My body jerks involuntarily, the contrast sending terrible shocks down my nervous system. My heart rate spikes, my breathing picks up, and Sarge is now in between Luke and I, blocking Luke's access to me with a snap of his teeth.

"I'm...I'm sorry," I respond. My visceral reaction to the contact has me confused, yet Luke's expression holds a hint of anger. At me? At the situation? "I don't know why I did that," I admit.

Is it possible that this is part of the remnants left behind from torture I can't remember? Will I be able to find answers? But, the better question might be, do I really want to go there?

Luke opens his mouth to speak, but it's not his voice that enters my eardrums. It's Mason's. "Amity," he calls from somewhere behind me. Before I turn, Luke's tensed muscles catch my attention. Mason has somehow weaseled his way in…again.

I rotate to see Mason walking toward us accompanied by a tall man with slicked back hair. His shoulders are square, his body looks rigid, but his demeanor is quite relaxed.

"Bonjour. I'm Olivier Favager. The General of the Human Protective Service," the man says, authority oozing from every word.

Mason's eyes are smiling, the deep blue sparkling as if they were clusters of gemstones shimmering in the sun. The General is someone he admires. "Mr. Favager is the one who sent for your extraction!"

Oh, why? What does this man want from me? And why did I need rescuing anyway? It's all so confusing. Torture, trackers, extractions, lies. Even…*death*. My head pounds with unanswered questions and distrust.

Luke's body heat is once again radiating from beside me. A sideways glance clues me in on how he's feeling. Something about what Mason has said doesn't sit right with him. *What else is new?* I mentally roll my eyes, but put a notch in it for later.

"We're glad to have you here. You're recovery is going well, I take it?" The General's voice lilts in a way that simultaneously makes me cringe, yet also empowers me.

"Y…yes," I say. "I thought tonight would be a good time to make an appearance. To pay my respects, of course."

"Of course, Miss Thorne. How admirable of you," he says.

The way he says my name—Miss Thorne—leaves my head reeling with panic. There's no reasonable explanation I can formulate for this response. The only thing I know for certain is that my gut is screaming at me, telling me something isn't right. Sarge is pressing into me so hard I fear I might fall over. God knows my body is already struggling as it is.

The General is regarding me with a curious eye. Is he expecting a thank you? For me to grovel at his feet and kiss his shoes? How can I thank a man if I don't know who the bad guy is here?

But I say, "I appreciate your kindness," anyway, because there is no reason to put myself on this man's bad side.

"You're very important to us, Miss Thorne," the General says. "It's good to see you're feeling better. Do have a good time." He nods and off he goes.

CHAPTER THREE　　　AMITY

SARGE IS PRESSED TO ME while I'm left trying to process my feelings. I've always told Emma never to ignore a gut feeling. But is it possible my brain is too damaged to distinguish anything these days?

"The fuck did you give him the credit for?" Luke seethes once the General is out of earshot.

Mason glares at him, looking around to make sure no one else has heard. But Luke's voice was so menacingly low that I barely heard it standing right next to him. "Keep your mouth shut, Warin," Mason warns. His voice isn't dark like Luke's, but it holds a similar command.

"Oh, that's right." Luke rolls his eyes. "I forgot this was Western America."

Before the tension of the conversation gets too thick, a voice in the crowd thankfully breaks it. "Amity!"

My whole body tenses in the struggle to find any recognition of this voice from my past. Unfortunately, there's nothing. I only recognize the voice from my last few weeks here.

I turn to find the one they call Lacy pushing her way through the crowd. Poor Sonya is trailing behind her, quietly apologizing for her girlfriend's rudeness. It makes me giggle.

"You look amazing!" Lacy says once she's closer. She puts her hands on my shoulders and keeps me at arm's length. "Absolutely stunning." I'm pulled in for a hug, and my body tenses once more.

Sarge offers his body weight against me, keeping his tail upright and wagging slightly. After a few minutes, he lets out a sharp crack of his teeth, and Lacy promptly pulls away.

"Sorry," she says, wiping her eye. "It's just…"

"It's alright," I mutter, casting my eyes down, brushing a loose strand of hair behind my ear. "You look great, too," I say after a few minutes of silence.

Lacy is wearing a tight pantsuit and blazer combo in a deep plum. She's stunning. Her black lob is perfectly styled, sitting just at her shoulders, and the matching purple of the tips accentuates her face. Her makeup is clean and crisp, making me look tired and naked in comparison.

"Thanks!" She's glowing. "But don't forget about Sonya!"

Sonya is in a chic lilac dress that cascades down her body in different layers. A thin slit barely lets her right leg peek out. The light color of the gown complements the dark of Lacy's. On their own, they are beautiful, but together? They're to-die-for.

"It's okay, baby," Sonya says. "You're the only one they'll notice."

Lacy pulls her in close, hugging her tightly. "Are you kidding me?" she says with a smile. "You are the star of the show, always."

Their words are bittersweet. Anyone looking on would swoon at the love they have, but I don't feel such happiness. All I can think of is how hurt they'd be if one of them were ripped away by this shitty society we're in. Or…were in. Maybe things could be different now that we're here with the H.P.S? *No Amity, you know that love is weakness.*

"Not to interrupt, but I actually think it's Sarge that steals the show," I say, hoping to stop the sappy displays.

Sarge sits proud, puffing out his chest. He's smug.

"Oh, yeah, little bro!" Lacy smiles. "You're killing it!"

Both Sonya and Lacy shower Sarge in pets. He's in dog heaven. I've never understood why Lacy calls Sarge "little bro", but that's on my list of things to find out. Perhaps Lacy and I were closer than I imagine.

The rest of the group makes introduction, but I'm not paying attention fully. Luke and Lacy are verbally sparring, and it's nice to be able to see him so natural and not uptight like he is in my presence. *I wonder if him and I were ever like this…*

"Thank you all for making our acquaintance here at this Grand Memorial Ball." An MC quiets the crowd with his sultry voice. "Please let us have a moment of silence for our fallen."

The people of the crowd simultaneously downturn their heads, bowing in silent prayer. Sarge rests his cheek against my hip, nuzzling close. He can sense my growing anxiety before I pinpoint it myself. I don't know why it's here, but it is.

"Thank you, everyone," the MC says. "Now please remain silent while our General delivers his speech."

And just like that, my anxiety is tenfold. My gut is screaming at me, telling me I'm not going to like what's coming next. I couldn't possibly ignore it even if I tried. The thought leads me to Emma. Oh, how I wish she were here and we were far away from this place.

"Hello citizens," General Favager addresses. "Let us make this night a beautiful celebration as we honor those not here with us today. Axom Hoover and Charlotte Bouchard have paid the ultimate price for our cause. But they will *not* die in vain." The look of determination on his face, the darkening of his eyes, is something I've seen many times in the Slums of Western America. A certain desperation for vengeance; for blood. "Would you all please open a space for Miss Amity Thorne?"

Hearing my name sends a jolt of angst throughout every nerve ending, knocking me from my thoughts. The heat in my face makes it nearly unbearable to breathe. The crowd creates a bubble of space around me, somehow knowing who I am amongst the sea of people.

"Miss Thorne is the key to our success. She is the one to rally our people. She is our call to arms. Mr. Hoover and Miss Bouchard died getting her to us, and what a sweet sacrifice it is. The Guardianship *will* fall now that she is in our corner. Tonight, we celebrate, for those we have lost have left us with the greatest gift of all."

The crowd erupts with cheers. Everyone is shouting with joy, though no one dares come closer than the bubble for fear of a teeth battle with my four legged companion.

My knees are weak, and I worry Sarge is the only reason I'm still upright. I didn't ask to be here, I don't even really know what *here* truly means. All I want is to be with my family. I don't want to be the key. I don't want to be anything!

All at once my brain projects an image of an older man with kind eyes. He tells me he doesn't know why people have decided I'm the key, but he knows there is light inside of me.

The memory is ripped from my head as fast as it was planted. I don't know the man's name, I don't recognize the pristine white of the backdrop, but the feelings building in my chest are all too familiar. The scene is surrounded with sadness and sorrow.

My teeth are clenched as I hit the ground, my hand finding a place on my skull to press away the pain. General Favager's voice carries through the hoard of bodies, seemingly getting closer and closer, yet still sounding miles from where I am. Someone calls to me, but I can't answer.

"Enjoy this night, for tomorrow brings not only a new day, but the dawn of a new era."

The clapping of hands is loud and harsh, but soon dulls into the background. All I hear is the beating of my heart and the bite of my hyperventilation. I need to get out of here. "Sarge," I gasp. "Go."

My weak fingers grip his fur tightly, and he braces himself to help me stand. With teeth barred, he releases a guttural snarl, daring anyone to get in his way. Every noise we make feels like it's a loud scream in the dead of night, but the truth is it's just a single drop in a massive ocean. The crowd tosses like waves, threatening to take me under. Thank goodness for Sarge. My lifesaver.

"Amity!" I hear my name again, but I'm unable to distinguish who is calling it. I don't want to be around anyone, anyway. I want to run.

Sarge and I collapse out into the hall and the cool ground beneath my knees offers a small slice of solace. Despite being in a thinly strapped dress, it seems the heat is consuming me. Sarge is working hard, trying to return me to reality. It's only a matter of time before Mason is behind me.

"What happened?" he asks.

"Give her a second," Luke seethes from somewhere nearby.

"I told you she shouldn't have left," Mason argues. This, I assume, is back at Luke.

"Or maybe she would've been fine if your jackass of a General didn't insinuate that she was responsible for the death of those soldiers," Luke spits in return.

"Well of course it wasn't her, it was their shithead of a leader!" Mason shouts.

"Luke!" Lacy shouts. Out of the corner of my eye, Luke can be seen lowering his fist back to his side, tightly pressing it in to keep it planted.

"Can you all just shut up!" I shout as loud as I can muster. "There's something going on here that no one is telling me, and I want to know what it is." I use Sarge's body to steady me as I stand up. The whirling in my head makes it hard to focus. My limbs are weak.

The other members of the group turn, completely shocked that I've spoken. Mason is the first to open his mouth. "We really should be getting you…"

"No!" I stomp my foot like an errant teenager, slightly losing my balance. "I want to know, now."

The other two are silent, but I'm begging them to speak up. Yet it's Mason who replies again.

"Your heartrate is getting too high, you need…"

"Stop deciding that you know what I need." My foot slips again, but I catch myself on Sarge. The heat in my face is back, but it's driving force is anger, not anxiety. "What I…" My voice stops working.

"Are you okay?" Lacy asks.

"I…need…" I speak the words, but the sentence isn't finished before the world around me is black, and the sensation of falling takes over.

"M!"

CHAPTER FOUR   LUKE

I LOOSEN MY TIE AS I open the door to my pod, dipping my head so I don't smack it off the ceiling. I walk slowly, casually sitting on the mattress, careful not to put all my weight onto the body that occupies it.

"Ack!" Sam cries, then giggles. His laughs are a needed melody tonight. Nothing with M seems to be going right.

"Oh, good," I say. "You're up!" I flip the switch and the light flickers on.

Sam covers his eyes with his hands—his real one, and the new skin modeled one that the Service gave him. If not for the robotic movements, I sometimes forget he only has one real arm. If only they had signal blocking ink when we needed it for Sam…

"I thought you were staying with your friends in Compound Two?" I question.

Sam and the other children in Mama June's care had been rescued by the Service while I saved M. Mama June is the fiery woman that risked her life daily to operate on the Tainted, giving them a chance at a better life. I'll never be able to repay her for taking in Sam like she did.

"I wanted to be here when you got back." His small voice tugs at my heart. I've never wanted anything more than for M to get better. The M I know would absolutely adore Sam. But the Amity that's here now isn't ready for the connection.

"Luckily for you, I came back alone and I don't need the bed." I smirk, suggestiveness laced throughout my tone.

"One, yuck. Two, I know you can't fit two adults in here!"

"Well, you don't really need a lot of space if you're…"

"La la la la la…" Sam puts his fingers into his ears.

I chuckle from deep in my gut. "Alright, alright." I reel him in. "It's late. We better get to bed." I've been given special permission to have Sam stay with me. Not that I didn't give them a hard bargain. I sure as hell wasn't going to deny Sam what he wanted, but staying in Compound Two was never an option. I need to be as close to M as possible. But in order for our arrangement to work, Sam gets the bed and I'm stuck with the floor. It sure does wonders for my back.

The light is turned off again and as we lay in silence, I listen to Sam's breathing. It hasn't slowed yet, not evened out. Something is bothering him. "Sam?"

Sam knows what I'm asking. He's smart. He skips the "what" and goes right into the issue. "I miss Sarge." Ah. With the return of M, Sarge hasn't let her out of his sight. That leaves Sam to mourn his friend, just like I'm mourning Amity. Then, "So it didn't go well on the Amity front?"

I sigh. "It was better than any other night," I answer honestly. I leave out the part about her passing out from stress, or whatever. I stayed just long enough to know she was okay, but then I left for fear of my fist kissing Mason's face. "I'm sorry about Sarge. I'm sure he's dying to see you."

"Yeah…" Sam says.

"Hey," I speak softly. "You know the second I can get you to see him, I will." I hate that he has to miss Sarge. My secret dream is for all of us to be happy together, without the external pressures of Western America. But it seems no matter where we are, there are too many forces beyond our control that won't let it happen. Instead I'm left with a broken dream and a crushed kid.

"Why do I have to wait?" Sam is confused. As much as I want to help him, we're both shit out of luck. Everything is a secret around here. And I'm none the wiser than a prisoner.

"I'm told it's because our presence might disrupt M's healing," I respond. Mason spews a lot of bullshit these days. Hell, just tonight he gave the General credit for my extraction idea. But after seeing what happened to M after that speech, maybe she *does* need some time.

"You believe that?" Sam asks. He knows when I'm giving a diplomatic answer.

I sigh. "I don't really know what to believe."

o o o

SAM HEADS OFF to meet his friends before class. Normally I'd be on my way to M's room already, to do the usual routine of getting kicked out within minutes, but today I've decided to wait. She needs her rest, and it's always good to throw a curveball once in a while.

I've requested a meeting with Cateline Pierre, the smartest scientist in all of the H.P.S., and maybe even the world. Her inventions have given the Service the upper hand on everything, including the extraction mission, and I'm hoping she'll be able to help with M's healing.

Cateline has practically been begging for a meeting since she saw me fight Axom with the STARS on. She wants to improve her algorithm. As it stands, it's an enhancement for the soldiers to give them an edge over their opponents. But like everything, it has its flaws.

Someone escorts me at 8:30. My Service clearance throughout the building is N.T.K.. Need to Know. This means I need someone with the highest clearance to take me most places. Personally, I think they have something to hide.

The Service has no doors, a juxtaposition for their clearly secretive practices. Sensors make it easy for the Service to identify people and if they belong where they are headed. Yet the deeper you get, the more obstacles you have to pass through. The truly restrictive areas are usually hidden by real doors, and may even have guarded security. Cateline's working quarters are a good example of this.

My escort nods to the two Service members blocking the entrance. The men step aside and I continue, alone, through the door. The room is massive, yet surprisingly empty. The few tables in the forefront of the room have various equipment that I don't concentrate on too much. Behind them, black mat flooring extends up, surrounding the entirety of the wall.

Cateline is leaning over a small object, intensely focused. She doesn't lift her head until I'm right next to her.

"Aha!" she exclaims. "Mr War...I mean...Luke." She smiles shyly.

Kudos to her remembering my aversion to the formality. "Cateline." I nod.

"Thank you for coming," she says. "I've been looking forward to getting in your head."

"Good luck." I smirk, but really I couldn't be further from playful. "It takes a lot."

"It can be simple to do with the right tools." The gleam in her eye matches the playful façade I've put forth.

I highly doubt that, lady, I think to myself. Ren had developed a way to see inside people's heads, and I found a way to shut it out. I'm able to compartmentalize even the nastiest of behaviors to not feel guilty. My brain is notorious for blocking everything.

"Come." She waves her hand for me to follow.

Cateline leads me toward the wide black mat. Her outstretched hand is in front of me when we stop. In it, a STARS device. Stabilizing Target and Range Simulator, or STARS, is a defensive advantage for those that wear it. It analyzes movement surrounding the wearer, giving them the ability to control their muscles in the special way they tell it to. The STARS requires knowledge of fighting, or at least quick thinking, without having to be physically trained in specific maneuvers.

I'll admit, it's a great idea. It levels the playing field for anyone that may want to volunteer for their cause here at the Service. But again—like everything—it has its weaknesses.

I place the STARS on my temple without question. It more than likely is already color matched to my skin due to the Chameleon Tech. Cateline is smiling when my gaze meets hers.

"Head to your place, please." She fans her hand outward in the desired direction.

There's a small mark in the center of the mat. My foot steps on it, and then I'm no longer alone. Different hologram bodies in a variety of different colors are now projected around me, all equidistant from me and each other. I spin around on my heel, returning my eyes to Cateline. "What's my objective?"

"Fight." She smiles.

The charged energy of the room excites me. The green body moves toward me first. It seems the others are staying in their place. Boo. One V One isn't excitable. So be it.

First, I'll have to decipher what type of fighter this AI is. More than likely, it's defensive. Though, who knows, Cateline could have made anything. Let's start with some light jabs.

Stepping forward, my right fist lifts, flying at half speed toward the face. At the last second, the AI shifts, sliding left. I do it again. The same result. The action brings me back to the first STARS experience I'd had with Axom. He is...was a very patterned fighter. Defensive rather than offensive. It's almost identical to the AI in front of me. That's when the rage takes over me.

Axom deserved a better leader. One that didn't let the emotions of reuniting with someone get the better of them. Screw the light jabs. I go into full fight mode, swinging, kicking, and spinning my way into the next opponent.

It starts in, almost no time to prepare. Scrambling forward, I meet the putrid yellow-green one by catching its punch mid-swing. Twisting the arm, I complete a rear wrist lock on it, making it nearly immobile right from the beginning.

The first had been fairly easy to drop. The second one, while more offensive, was still just as effortless in stopping. This next one, a bright yellow, is already putting up more of a fight than its fully and mixed green counterparts. This one retaliates every third throw. Still too patterned for my taste. But then, it clips me.

Fuck. The pressure against the side of my head pisses me off. Though, I only have myself to blame. I got lax. The fucker had thrown a fist at two, rather than three. I had moved only as fast as I could, just barely making it, but not before the robotic knuckles scraped against my temples.

It's almost like they're learning. I physically shake my head to restart fresh. This time, I circle behind the AI and bring it to the ground by launching onto its back. I don't release the chokehold until its limp.

In similar fashion as before, the next in line leaves no time before closing the distance. It doesn't immediately go in for a hit, but it expertly dodges and retaliates after mine.

This one is more experienced than the last, which had been better than the one before that. They've been getting more offensively smart with each new opponent. Color must have a correlation to skill. Which already makes this a fool's practice.

As the thought completes itself in my head, the remaining bodies run in circles around me while their colors muddle into a matching deep purple. Interesting.

The one in front of me morphs into the same shade just as quickly. Then, it promptly boots into an amazingly precise offensive maneuver, leaving me to dip, dive, and glide away from everything with very little time or energy to spare for my own attacks. Even with my mind controlling the STARS, the throws don't land. The AI is quick to pull away and continue its beating.

It's slowly backing me into a corner. If it succeeds, I may be toast. I could, in theory, use the wall to my advantage. But the timing would have to be perfect. Between the flying fists and kangaroo kicks, my focus is tied up in front of me. Out of my peripheral, I'm hoping to catch a glimpse of something that could help. There's nothing, though. It's just me, the mat, and the plum colored bodies.

Wait. That's it! The air in front of me continues its onslaught of attacks, and I bide my time, letting it back me up. Last second, just as we pass by the stoic fighters awaiting their turn, I dip low, spinning, slamming the body to my right up onto my shoulders. On the turn back to 360, the body slides with the momentum of the turn and I swing it like a baseball bat, taking out the one in front of me. Both of them crash to the mat and melt away like the previous ones.

The last of them starts in now, and I let it close some distance before I turn, running. It picks up speed behind me to catch up. Perfect.

The wall is directly in front of me, and a tilt of my head tells me the AI is basically at my heels now. I swear the fucker has a smile on its face despite not having any facial features. That's when I launch, diving into the wall, pushing myself up and over the body barreling toward me. I land behind it, and in its moment of hesitation, I slam its head into the wall. Repeatedly. Voraciously. Letting all the built up anger from the last few weeks out in a guttural scream, until the AI turns to ash beneath my fingers.

My breathing is ragged when I turn to a wide-eyed scientist. Cateline's mouth hangs slightly open. Damn it, Warin, you've let the monster out. But her words are not what I imagine.

"That...was...amazing!" She's excited? "You have helped tremendously!"

"Helped?" I laugh. I knew I was coming for her to pick my brain, but I don't see how this could have helped her at all.

"Of course." She smiles. "The STARS collected your thoughts."

"My..." Oh... My voice fades, my lips forming an "o" shape without any noise. "You sly devil." I smirk.

Cateline blushes. "I've not had anyone beat that test before, Luke. This will help me analyze what makes you different."

A frown presents itself on my face. What makes me different? The intruding voice of my brain tells me it's the monster that lurks just below the surface. I push it away. "I've deduced that the STARS is only as good as the fighter it's attached to."

"Correct," Cateline agrees. "A fighter of sound brain will utilize the STARS in ways one can only dream about."

Cateline proceeds to share a story of a soldier they lost because he was not mentally stable and the STARS had taken his deeply disturbed intrusive thoughts and made them reality. His emotions had somehow pushed things too far. He ended up hurting his partner and quite literally tore himself apart. She dampened some of the effects of the STARS after that, but wants to improve without having consequences.

"It was brutal," she says, sighing. "The mind is fickle."

"That is exactly why Service training should involve critical thinking and problem solving in real world applications," I suggest. "If they focus only on physical training, the soldiers will fall short." It's surprising that no one has come to this conclusion yet. I'd bested Axom on the mat without any form of STARS on because he simply didn't have the capacity to analyze the situation. He was a skilled fighter indeed, yet his mind was his weakness.

Cateline regards me curiously. "Perhaps I will adjust the algorithm to analyze patterns, not just movement in general. I can give these soldiers an upper hand by letting them know the type of fighter they are up against." She touches her dainty fingers to her chin in thought. Then she smiles again, meeting my eye. "I'm glad to have met you," she says.

Compliments don't penetrate the tough exterior I've built up over the years. I wouldn't believe it anyway. Not even from Amity. Speaking of...

"What do we have in helping Amity recover her memories?" I ask, flipping the topic of conversation.

Cateline's face drops subtly. "Mr... Luke," she corrects. "We've done everything."

Tsk. Tsk. "Cateline," I say, dropping my voice low, leaning in close. The hitch of her breath clues me in on the power I hold. Gotcha. "You're telling me you haven't thought of anything else? You? Cateline Pierre?" A smirk plays at my lips. It's harder to push the thoughts out of my head than expected. This is wrong, but I'd do anything for Amity.

Cateline's face flushes a pastel pink, and her eyes flutter in that way that most people's do when they're being flattered. "Luke," she breathes. "I'm not all that great with the biological side of things." Her words are tinged with double meaning.

"You're being humble," I state, pushing further. "I'm sure you could think of something." One more killer smile and I think it's secure.

Color rushes to her cheeks once more. "I will try," she breathes.

"Thank you," I say before walking out.

Once in the hall, I attempt to distance myself from who I just was in my mind. Sometimes we have to do things that make us questionable individuals. I've done it my whole life. It's easy for me to play on people's weaknesses because I'd learned from the best.

The thought of Ren sours my mood even more. So much so that I almost pass my escort in a rage. Fuck this slow ass. The only thing I want right now is to see M. Somehow that will make everything better. Maybe it's just my guilty conscience talking, which—relatively speaking—is a win, because until I met her, I didn't think I had one.

The escort leaves me once we're in the Commons, the central location that everyone has access to. It is a gigantic circle room with a massive statue of the of the Service's emblem. Resembling an angel, a *savior*, the individual with wings outstretched is nearly fifty feet tall. For being underground, it's quite impressive.

Above the statue is a faux dome skylight. Since we're underground, the Service projects an image of a beautiful blue sky. It emits UV rays, curtesy of Cateline Pierre's extravagant mind. Basically it's the closest thing to a real window without actually being one. And since the weather is always sunny, the statue consistently has a heavenly glory about it as the rays peer down in a halo of gold.

The Commons is a meeting place for the residential ward. It's the location that connects all others.

So instead of veering left toward the pods, I keep straight. I'm on a mission to see M and nothing will stand in my way. The hospital ward in and of itself is a mini version of the Commons. There is one central point with all of the rooms spanning from there. It's a small place, what with all of the advancements here. Yet, it's proven helpful—somewhat—in the odd case of M.

The light at the end of the tunnel-like hallway is as bright and harsh as ever. Only this time when I step over the threshold into the fluorescents, I find myself stuck. Literally.

A high pitched siren blares, no doubt causing a ruckus for the six patients of the ward. The nurse behind the counter shakes her head as she lifts the phone to her ear.

"Unauthorized access," says a prerecorded voice. "Lucas Paul Warin."

Son of bitch! When I get my hands on that slimy weasel Mason Baines, I swear he'll be needing a room here if he survives. That lousy, no good, piece of…

"Luke." His voice fills my head when I absolutely do not want it to. The worst part is I still can't move. Which means I still can't see him. Or hurt him. Lucky Mason.

Even though I want to shout, I can't. I'm unable to move my mouth as well. How convenient. He's doubly lucky. For now.

His stocky frame rounds into my view. The cocky demeanor he carries sends me overboard, but my body doesn't outwardly show it, because it can't. I've no doubt my face is red with rage, though. Explosive anger is building, scrambling to the surface, searching for release.

"I'm going to allow you to talk, but if you get loud, I'll shut you right back up," he cautions, as though I'm an errant toddler. Fuck this guy.

Mason waits a few seconds, like he's waiting for a confirmation, before realizing I can't fucking move. It takes another second before my mouth is able to open. "What the fuck is this?" The words sneak through my teeth in seething anger.

"Protocol," Mason snips.

"Bullshit!" I say louder than intended.

Mason widens his eyes in warning, tilting his head and lifting the button in his hand. "It is protocol," he reiterates. "As of yesterday."

"What could possibly be the reasoning for this?" I question. Every day that I spend here, the more I fear the Service and its leaders are like Western American and Ren. Or at the very least, they've got something big they're hiding, and M plays into it somehow. Why else would they go through all these hoops to keep her in the dark?

"I'm going to skip the formalities and jump right into it," Mason starts.

"Oh, please do," I goad, a tight expression on my face.

His body tenses, then relaxes as he says, "It's your fault, jackass. There. You happy?"

"My fault?" I stare at him in disbelief. Mostly because I still can't move my head to look away.

"Yes!" His voice is louder than before. "You knew you weren't allowed here and yet you argued with it every day; disobeying direct orders from your superior."

"My superior?" Ha! I laugh out loud at his joke. He really believes himself to be above me? Maybe in the Service, but never in matters where M is involved.

"She should have never known about the Memorial Ball!" He looks at me, a slight begging tone to his voice. "It's your fault she even left the safety of this hospital." There's something more to it than this. The General was more than pleased to see M out and about. If this is Mason's doing, then I'll have to push his buttons.

"You mean the confines of this prison?" I spit, correcting him.

Mason takes a step back as if physically jolted by my words. "We're doing what's best for Amity," he says. "Unlike you, who seems to only do whatever it is that best suits yourself."

I open my mouth to speak again, but a sweet sound fills the air instead. M.

"I want to see him," she says.

"Amity," Mason starts. "You need…"

"No!" The harsh bite of her words startles even me. It's clear the glower in her face is taking all of her energy. "Stop telling me what I need. You don't know anything about me." She crosses her arms. Sarge sits quietly by her side, steadying her.

"You may not remember, but I do know you." Mason sighs. "And it might be hard to understand, but this is all for your safety…"

She scoffs. "If you're going to force me to stay in this prison cell of a hospital, then you're going to allow visitors."

Mason opens his mouth to speak, but then shuts it. He casts his eyes away, battling with himself. I'd hate to have been M's father when she was a teen. Right now, she's developmentally in that stage, but thankfully there aren't any hormones to make it worse.

Somehow I'm able to keep myself quiet. Despite the rage radiating with every pulse at the sight of Mason, I need to let M fight her battles on her own. She's always been headstrong. She just needs to learn her own power again.

In the midst of the showdown, a nurse scurries over to Mason. The look on his face is determination set with resignation.

After an intense whispering match, Mason's breath releases in another sigh. "Fine." M's shoulders drop with relief, but its subtle. Mason doesn't notice, though he's already facing me. He walks close, knowing full well I can't do anything to hurt him. Coward. "Keep your mouth shut, Warin. Or I'll have no choice." He shoves past me before clicking the button to fully release me. Fuckhead.

CHAPTER FIVE REN

"DAMN IT!" MY FIST SLAMS against the rich mahogany of my desk.

Marcus Giles, my first sergeant, is sitting uncomfortably in the furniture at our sky offices in the heavily fortified Capital of Western America. Now that Omphalos has been destroyed, and most of my patients are gone, the plan to save Humanity took the fast track to nowhere. I need to replenish my Exceptionals in the off chance the ones I had haven't survived. We were only able to get a few before the collapse. The frozen reserves are tempting, but that's still not enough. The time isn't right.

"The numbers for this week are as pathetic as that look on your face." The files fly from my hand, tossing them away from me. Marcus sits up now.

"We will find them," he assures.

I scoff, causing him to flinch. The problem is, nearly 95% of the Commoners we've tested so far are too much like that vile girl, Miss Thorne. Thanks to the scan of her brain, we're able to deem a person tainted almost instantaneously. We can give them a score on how likely they are to change, but until we have a main facility where I can keep a close watch, we're stuck in the water. Besides, there have hardly been any new candidates.

"There are still plenty of other locations with non-tainted individuals." Marcus won't stop. "Sure, the Exceptionals may be gone, but we can…" It's at this point he looks at me to find the scowl on my face. His voice fades into nothing.

"The ones we have should be safely secure under the shield, but unless we get to them soon, they'll starve to death." My eyebrows pull in at my words.

Marcus had projected the protective shield to save those on the inside of Omphalos when it started to fall. A safety protocol proven most worth it. However, there's been some unrest from the squads that lost their officer comrades.

"Are any of the Tainted good matches for subcopies?" Marcus questions in an attempt to distract me.

Are any of the Tainted good matches for subcopies? My inner bitch sneers. I admire Marcus' loyalty, but he damn sure gets on my nerves. Like a lost puppy.

"None," I spit. "Hence, the damn it."

Marcus recoils, cowering into himself again. I understand he thinks he's being helpful, but the truth is, he's just reminding me of all this failure. I didn't come all this way, sacrificing everything, to fail.

Despite the lack of bodies to use, there is good in all of this. It's only a matter of time before my precious son will be back with me.

Not only is Miss Thorne's brain scan helping us weed out the rotten, it is also helping me find ample hosts for a little side plan to get my sweet Lucas out of her clutches. For those with a 96%, or better, brain match, they are physically reconstructed to resemble Miss Thorne, and the memories I have of hers are downloaded into what we're calling subcopies.

Since that little raid of Omphalos caused me to act in ways I hadn't originally intended, the new goal is that I get Lucas to fall in love with one of these other ones, thus convincing him to return to me. I held out hope that my other plans would work, but love is a stupid fickle thing. He's my son, though, damn it, and if he's going to be dumb enough to fall, then I'm going to do my best to make sure it's with someone made more easily agreeable. Subcopies have proven useful in the past, so why not for this as well? Gah, the things a mother does for her child.

Along with that, we're also able to learn more about the human mind, which has always been an interest of mine. By implanting Miss Thorne's memories into other individuals, we will be able to study if experience affects people, or overall genetics. It's the age old question: Nature or Nurture. And these studies will live on. At the very least, my name will go down in history somewhere.

"We still have more to test, Headmistress," Marcus reassures, his eyes the size of saucers. "Hope is not yet lost."

Hope. The word is revolting. The last thing we want is hope. My fingers reach the bridge of my nose, pinching the irritation out of my brain. Marcus is extra insufferable lately since out little spat in the presence of that vile girl. He had questioned my motives, my decisions. As if being a protective mother is such a terrible thing.

"You are dismissed, Mr. Giles," I sigh.

His eyes hold the sad puppy look for a split second before he nods, removing himself from the room.

After a moment of silence, I reach for the Relay on my desk. Master Sergeant Dean Carovak is speaking just a few moments later. "Yes, Headmistress?"

"Mr. Carovak," I start. "How are you this morning?"

"The rubble is almost completely cleared from the East Wing, Madame," he answers, knowing I wasn't asking about him personally. Sometimes I fear I'd made a mistake promoting Marcus over Dean, but regret is not something I can afford. If I weren't saving Sergeant Major for my son...

"And the unrest?" I question, not letting my mind wander. Marcus had been too coward to tell me, but the rigidness of the Force is beginning to wane. Those caught beneath the shield need to be freed, lest we only pull dead bodies from the cracked earth. The problem is, everything on top needs to be cleared away first.

"A few more lost it today, Madame," he answers. "I've heard from some of the other Masters dealing with unruly ranks as well."

Crap.

The sigh slips past my lips before I can stop it, my forehead pressing against the side of my fist. The officers are losing faith in the plan. They are upset about the lost lives in Omphalos. The ones under the direct order of Mr. Carovak are acting out the worst. They are the ones assigned to clean up duty after all.

But they are stupid. Incapable of seeing the bigger picture. The longer they take, the more they risk those still alive at the bottom to suffer a terrible death. They just have to push through the top layers to get through. They are weak.

"If it not be out of turn," Mr. Carovak starts. "May I offer some advice?"

Normally something like this would irritate me, but today it is miniscule compared to everything else that is going on. "Speak," I say, swirling my hand as if he were here, before returning my forehead to it.

"Perhaps, Madame," he begins, before stopping to clear his throat. He's hesitant. "Perhaps you make a spectacle."

My head lifts as if this idea had just popped into it on its own. That's it. That's exactly what needs to be done. Strike a bit of fear. "And who do you suggest?" I'm asking for the worst offender; the officer that will show the others exactly why they don't want to step out of line.

"I'll have a report to you by the end of day," he states.

"Thank you, Mr. Carovak," I say. "As always, it's been a pleasure." The Relay clicks as our communication ceases. Then, Marcus is immediately on the line.

"Yes, Headmistress?" His eager voice is sickening.

"Marcus," I say. "Get in here, I've got a plan."

o o o

MARCUS IS SPEAKING gingerly to Master Sergeant Dean Carovak as the A.L.F. officers shuffle nervously into formation. Marcus doesn't hold the same confidence that his inferior does, and instead seems to shrink beside Dean. Damn it. I knew it was a mistake to choose Marcus Giles.

"Mr. Carovak," I say, stepping in. "Your men look restless."

Something familiar flashes in Dean's eye. Recognition? Yes. He understands I'm keeping Marcus from making a fool of himself in front of the watchful eyes of the low ranking Force. They'll pick out any weakness and use it. I can appreciate that on a fundamental level, but not when it goes against my order. *My* order.

"They are," Mr. Carovak agrees. "Not only are we dealing with the same issues discussed yesterday, my officers are on edge about your surprise visit."

His expression gives nothing away as he mentions the word *surprise*. Every minute I spend talking to Dean, I realize what a fool I'd been to leave him as a Master Sergeant. But perhaps it's for the betterment of running his A class squad.

"Yes," the word slips from my lips. "Things will be rectified shortly." The sinister smile on my face is enough to make whispers scatter through the crowd. My eyes flick to the closest officer in line and he instantly tenses, looking blankly forward. This is going to be fun.

"Are you ready, Mistress?" Marcus asks.

A curt nod is all he receives from me. The small device he'd been holding is now pressed onto the space where my neck meets my chin. I step forward, shedding the two men beside me. The further they are behind me, the less they'll shadow my authority.

"Hello everyone." My sinister voice is low, carrying beautifully over the crowd thanks to the amplifier under my chin. "Some of you may be wondering why I've made an impromptu visit."

The squirms of several members in the formation jolts my heart with excitement. Their discomfort, their fear; it sends pulses of energy through me.

"Would any of you like to guess?" The corner of my lip turns up in a playful smirk. I always have enjoyed a good game. The mischievous look in my eye can only truly be seen by those in the first few rows.

There's a good hundred men here. The twenty-five squad members under the direct leadership of Dean Carovak and three additional outside squads brought in as time ticked away. Those trapped below the surface of the collapsed mountain are running out of food and air as we speak. This is a waste of precious opportunity to save my Exceptionals, but it must be done.

Not-so-shockingly, no one speaks up. Why would they? Even if they know the reason I'm here, they wouldn't so much as dare to open their mouths. Perhaps they are *all* guilty?

"It appears a handful of your squad mates have been getting…" I pause to find the right word. "Rowdy," I finally decide on. "Some are refusing the order we so desperately need to uphold."

At this point, my legs have carried me closer to line one. The officers near the direct center are sweating bullets as I close the distance.

"How can we stop the Commoners from an uprising if we can't even keep control of ourselves?" My voice is faux woeful.

The man in front of me gulps. He's nearly shaking, as he should be. This officer may just be nervous over my domineering presence. Or, he's suddenly hyper-aware that he's my target.

Officer Harlow Jacobs. Recruited around the same time as my sweet Lucas. First in almost all of the squads he's been assigned to, yet he's never shown interest in climbing the ranks. Though, he's a natural leader amongst his fellow officers I've heard. Hence why his increasing attitude toward authority is an issue. It's unfortunate such talent must be wasted, but that is the cost.

The special immobilizing device is in my hand and pressed against Mr. Jacobs neck in a millisecond. Pulling him from formation and further from the crowd, I'm finally able to see the worried expressions of his comrades' faces.

"Mr. Jacobs," I say, "has been ousted as the worst offender of breaking order. And for that? He will pay."

Marcus and Dean step forward, each taking one arm of Harlow Jacobs as I release my immobilizing hold on him. His breathing climbs to a ragged state as some semblance of control resumes throughout his body. Fool. You don't need air where you're going.

"Anything you'd like to say?" I toy.

He shakes his head sharply. Mr. Jacobs has accepted defeat. Smart, yet an imbecile all the same.

"Very well."

Rope cuffs around Mr. Jacobs' wrists extend into taut lines held by Marcus on one side and Dean on the other. They need to keep their distance for what's about to happen.

I, too, step away. Not closer to the crowd, but further, so that Mr. Jacobs is in between. This way I'll be able to see the crowd's reaction as well.

Pulling yet another handy tool from my arsenal, the detonator is ready and waiting in my palm. After Lucas ran, I implanted every Force officer with a tracker, just like my patients. One wrong move, one step toward somewhere they aren't supposed to be and *bang*.

I've only ever had to threaten this before. Thankfully, yet sadly, I've never had to use it. Until today.

The formation of officers is shifting like the waves of a sea in turmoil. This way, and that; churning with restless energy. Those who were unaware, or were willfully ignorant, can no longer hope for a different outcome now that the all-too-famous detonator is in my hand. The only thing that would make this better would be to have Lucas do the honors.

My brow pulls in at the slight souring of my mood. Lucas will be back soon. But not if I have a broken regime. The task at hand brings me back, separating myself from the sad mother persona. It's time.

"Let this be a reminder," I address the crowd. "Order and chaos cause destruction. To yourself, to others, to society as a whole." I've always loved a good monologue. Speeches about order are necessary to the rallying cause. "There will be no more disarray. For not only is it bad practice, and is leaving your brethren under this stone for far too long, but it would make Mr. Jacobs' death a poor one. Do not sully his passing. He is the cost today. Let this be the end."

My thumb presses the button it had so smoothly been caressing during the speech. Mr. Jacobs' body melts into itself, so it appears. The tracker releases a specially formulated toxin into the bloodstream, heating the victim from the inside out. Harlow Jacobs' body convulses and he pulls inward, trying to scratch the heat from under his skin.

After a few seconds, the blood in his veins turns black, and he combusts. The human body cannot sustain internal temperatures above 104 for very long. By 122, they've definitely shut down. This toxin shoots my officers up to 150.

The blast of guts and sludgy black blood isn't large. A five foot radius is all that's left of Harlow Jacobs.

Just when I think we've settled things, a voice breaks from the sea of people. "He was a good man!" Someone pushes forward, racing their way to me. Mr. Carovak has him held steady in a second flat.

"You'll soon be wishing you'd kept your mouth shut, soldier," says Mr. Carovak through his teeth.

"Why? She'll kill me like she did Harlow? I'm not scared!" His eyes betray him as I get close. Such an insignificant rat. He has a point, though. Being able to play on everyone's weakness is what gives me the edge I need. I'm not so naïve to believe that all humans are afraid of Death. Some souls are too far gone for that. So perhaps what happens next will help clear the air.

My voice is menacingly low, yet amplified tenfold as those around hush to hear. I'm certain this young officer feels the icy chill of my breath as I say, "A good man is a quiet one. It's best you learn that lesson quickly."

Pulling clippers from my belt of many tools, I order Marcus and Dean to hold open the poor sap's mouth. His eyes are wide, tears soaking his cheeks. The onlooking officers are holding their breath as the nasty metal slams against his tongue. The pink flesh drops to the dirt and I kick it to the side with my heel.

"Clean this up," I order Mr. Carovak.

The soldier has pools of crimson streaming down his chin. His face is devoid of color. The audience behind him is trying to hold their stomachs. Some look away in fear, others keep their gaze for the same reason.

"Get back to work," Giles shouts at the men. He turns to me with a smile. "This went well, yes?" he asks.

"Yes, Marcus," I answer with a smirk. "I think these children know exactly how to behave now."

Made in the USA
Columbia, SC
15 September 2024